Proxy O

C000130042

An Erotic Story Of What My Son Is Missing (Guilty

Secret)

Camila Hudson

it wasn't bought for your personal use only, go back to your favorite ebook retailer and buy your copy. Thank you for acknowledging this author's efforts.

Table of Contents

Content Warning

Due to its sexual content, this book is only for those over the age of legal adulthood. There are some topics with a lot of foul languages. All of the characters are at least eighteen years old.

Introduction

Your son don't know how much he's missing out on his mom – Rita

What a dream come through to take all of my son in me – Ella

Note: this is for people in the age bracket 18+

Proxy Of My Son

"What do you think?"

He was now closely examining my appearance as if he were a judge at a prestigious beauty pageant. He'd already chosen to vote for me based on the expression on his face, and I was thrilled to see that

What I'm saying is, "Slowly turn around so I can see you all."

Then I continued to do so. That brought a smile to his face.

It was enough to say, "THANK YOU."

I was dizzy when I came to a halt, but I was able to remain motionless. After all, he'd had plenty of time to think about what he wanted to say. As soon as I asked him the question again, I knew exactly what he was going to say.

Because he'd said, "Perfect!" as expected, I was correct.

Both of us burst out laughing at the mere mention of the phrase. Anyone who saw us would have thought we were insane.

Ella: Hello, I'm Ella, and I'd want to introduce myself to you, Park. For the past 22 years, we've been together, but we're not married. We may one day get married, but for the time being, we're content to live our lives in sin. Why mess with a good thing that's already working? If something isn't broken, why fix it?

We've been playing this little game for years whenever I'm getting ready to go out, whether it's with him or one of my friends. It never fails to delight us.

What does he think of my appearance?

Because he loves me, his response is always the same. His response is always, "Perfect," even when I am anything but perfect.

What's more, no matter what my appearance is, he always responds the same way, as if he truly believes what he says, and it always sounds sincere. That puts me even more in love with him.

We don't because I'm too scared to try. I'm not a fragile egoist who needs him to say it to me to boost my self-worth. As far as I'm concerned, I'm worth more than I give myself credit for. In addition, it's not because I'm unattractive and rely on him to tell me I'm desirable. Even though I'm 42, I'm still approached by young males asking for my phone number. Even though it makes me happy, I always respectfully decline. My bond with Park is everything that matters to me.

So, why do we go through with such a pointless ritual? It's a no-brainer. We do it because we enjoy it, and that's a perfectly valid reason!

My best buddy, Rita, and I were planning a night out tonight. Compared to me, she is ten years younger. I wanted to look my best because she is always so well-dressed and well-groomed, so I wanted to do the same. The last thing I did before leaving was to check my appearance in the mirror. The best word to describe my appearance would be "amazing."

I'm a work of art. This may come off as arrogance, but it is not. Simply stated, this is the case. There are many people who say that my eyes are the deepest shade of blue they've ever come across. There is no room for disagreement here. My eyelashes are also lengthy. I think that's a successful formula. Flickering my eyes when I see a man makes me want him more. It should be enough for any woman, but I'm fortunate because I have more to give. In addition to my wide lips, I have a small nose that perfectly complements my facial shape. These are lips that were made to be kissed, or even better, to be serviced by a hot cock. Short golden hair adorns the face I'm most proud of. Also, in case you're wondering, yes, I am a born blonde!

My body, on the other hand, must either match my face or be an embarrassment. The fact that all of my female friends are envious of it makes me happy. To go along with my enormous breasts, I've got ample hips and a flat stomach. Despite the fact that I'm not a size zero, I am a woman. I'm a woman of great proportions. A man walking behind me will most likely be staring down at my rear end because I constantly walk with my hips wagging.

My turn came to drive, and that meant I had to go pick up Rita. For once, when I arrived at her place fifteen minutes early, I found her fully dressed and ready. We both burst out laughing as soon as we spotted each other. We both wore the same clothing. dressed in a red miniskirt and white blouse. We even had red handbags that matched our

11

outfits.

The next question on her mind was, "Where shall we go?"

I checked the time on my wristwatch. The park was closed because it was too early in the morning.

My turn at the back of the pack in the woods.

She nodded her head, and we headed off on our journey. We couldn't wait to get there, and so could you. In other words, what were we, two well-dressed, attractive ladies, going to be doing in the woods anyway?

We had decided to go dogging.

Rita wasn't lying to everyone because she was unmarried, but I was because I had Park. It doesn't matter what you think of my actions, so long as you don't tell Park I don't give a damn.

I'm a dog lover, and it's a secret I'm happy to share!

12

I was starting to feel thrilled as we neared our destination. In anticipation of what was going to happen once we arrived, my heart was racing and my pussy-muses were moistening rapidly.

It was nine inches long, but she managed to get it all into her petite pussy. "I hope that gentleman with the large cock is back again," she said with pride in her voice.

Although I wanted to chuckle because her pussy could take a cock that large, I managed to retain a serious expression on my face. In contrast to her, I had no interest in the size of her breasts. Seven inches is the right size for me because they're more manageable. You know, I'm not going to turn away a well-endowed man, but I'm not going to let him utilize all of his cock.

My favorite parking spot was still available as we neared the Dogging site, so I pulled in.

There were four vehicles in total, including mine. As far as I could tell, six males were standing next to them. It was a lot more crowded than normal.

Two of them began walking toward us as soon as I exited the vehicle to get into the back seat. When they arrived at the car, I had the door closed and the windows up. My window was tapped by one of them.

"Are you two ladies seeking for cock?" he asked with a wide smile when it was down.

I knew that was a foolish question, but I couldn't tell him so out of respect for him. Was about to answer, but Rita stepped in and saved the day.

"Yes, and we aren't ladies," she replied.

We were all in stitches.

Time to get together and work together. Rita lowered her

window as the second man approached the vehicle. All of us were glancing at each other without any subtlety. Rita started the conversation.

She said, "I want you," pointing at the man who'd inquired if we were seeking a cock.

We could tell by his wide smile that he was overjoyed to have her. What about me, though? In the same way, I would have preferred him. In truth, he was the most attractive and muscular of the two men, and he was taller and more imposing. They were all of a certain age. She was in her thirties, whilst I was somewhere between a teen and a twenties. When I was 42, I could legally be considered his mother. Instead, I would have preferred him to be older and more crucially, to not resemble my 19-year-old Son in any way. We were still going to have sex despite my reservations, so he should not be concerned.

They had now joined us in the automobile. I was able to

see him plainly because the interior lights were on. He had an eerie resemblance to Paul. A casual observer would mistake him for my son if he had his hair dyed darker and his nose shaved shorter.

"What's your age?"

"Nineteen."

He said, "I have a son the same age as you."

My stomach was in a knot. When I arrived at the Dogging site, I had no intention of meeting someone who might be my son.

"You're stunning," he says.

He meant it, and I knew it. He then placed his palm on my face, and I felt goosebumps rising my spine.

"Do you mind if I kiss you a little?"

That was never going to fly. I only kissed Park because he

was the one I adored. I didn't come for a romantic evening with a partner; rather, I came for some anonymous sex. For reasons I could not understand, I said yes this time.

A torrent of my blood flowed when he kissed me fiercely, and when our lips connected my fluids began to flow. My genitals were oozing with wetness.

His hands were squeezing and groping against my breasts. I didn't mind that he was hard on me.

They were already fucking and I was trying to ignore the noise from the front of the car. It didn't matter, though. I was so engrossed in what this young man was doing to me that I couldn't care less about the rest of the world. My man is the one I'd like to trade for him before, but now I have no intention of doing so. As amazing as this was, I knew it would only get better from here on out.

He'd taken my blouse and bra off with dexterity and

quickness I'd never seen before from someone his age. He was taking advantage of the fact that I was unable to stand on my own two feet. He had one nipple on his lips and the other in his fingers as he sucked passionately. A woman's breasts made him feel as though he had never experienced them before.

Things took a turn for the worse after that. I tried to put a stop to it, but I was unable. My desire to continue with the experience only grew stronger as time went on. After all, I'd started to worry about my Son, and now I wasn't with a stranger who looked like him anymore; I was with him. My beloved Paul was having a good time with my enormous genitalia. The more I wanted him to do it, the more I wanted him to do it immediately.

What does Mummy's pussy say to Paul?

He did, and he didn't even have to remove my underwear. With a swift pull to the side and three fingers up to the knuckles later, I had his attention. I was almost tempted to come. That was followed by him using them on me. At that point, I no longer considered myself a human being but rather an animal. A sex-crazed wild animal.

But his reign of terror was about to come to an abrupt end. My plan was to seize control.

"Fuck me hard, get your cock out."

He'd been surprised when I'd yelled it at him.

"Please, don't make me repeat myself."

After a murmured apology, he went right back to doing my bidding.

He slipped a rubber on his cock as soon as it was out. The extra time I had allowed him to take a closer look at it and determine what was in store for my pussy.

In that state of mind, I wouldn't have had any issues

accepting a large cock, and I would have happily eaten it all up. Although his was a small one, perhaps only five inches long, he still had a lot of fun with it. My enthusiasm was at an all-time high and that would be more than enough to put me out for the night.

My panties had been removed and I'd been pushed up high by him before he entered me. They had gotten so close to the car's roof that they were able to touch it.

Let's call me Mummy instead of fucking around.

The second strike was harsher than the first one. The next was even better.

"Would Mummy approve?"

Of course, I did, but he was a young man, so he could give me more. Furthermore,

"Harder."

Now the car was rocking.

"Faster."

However, it required a second strike from him to knock me off my feet.

My entire body was suddenly submerged in a huge climax. Even my toes started to curl up. I closed my eyes when I was at its climax. I observed him re-inserting his cock into his jeans as soon as I opened them when my ordeal was finished.

"Thanks," and then, as he was about to open the door, "I'm Tom. I am not Paul," he replied while smirking. It's time to tell your son what he's missing."

He walked away as I stood there and observed. That's when I saw what he was holding in his hand. He'd taken a keepsake, something to remind him of our brief acquaintance. Those were my red pants. Even though they weren't expensive, I wish he'd taken the used condom with him instead of leaving it on the back seat for me to handle.

We've stayed for second helpings before, but tonight was not one of those nights. We were both satisfied with our intercourse, so we decided to call it a night.

The drive back to Rita's house was unpleasant. She'd finished before me, so she'd heard a lot of what had been spoken in the rear of the car. She was having a ball taunting me by mimicking our voices and repeating what she'd heard.

What does Mummy's pussy say to Paul?

That was a total flop on my part. I still didn't know why I'd said what I did.

"Would Mummy approve?"

But I wish she'd stop talking about it. I'm glad she did, but when I dropped her off at her apartment she couldn't help·but say anything else.

Your son doesn't know how much he's missing out on, so tell him.

I didn't join in on her laughter when she did. As I drove away, I made a point of keeping a low profile and remaining silent.

When I returned, Park was fast sleeping. I jumped into bed with him after a quick shower. I thought about my life and how fortunate I was to have a companion as understanding as he was as I snuggled up to him.

Because he's a clever person and doesn't know I go Dogging, he must think I'm doing something wrong. Whatever it is, he always respects my privacy and never inquires about it. He allows me to maintain my secret because he cares about me. Not many men would do that, therefore I consider myself fortunate.

Paul surprised us with a visit over the weekend, which was a pleasant surprise.

"I hope it's okay with you? I figured this would be a good place to spend my two weeks of study break."

Mind? Both of us were ecstatic about the outcome of the transaction. In the meantime, I was making his room ready. Having him back home was going to be great.

The last time we'd seen him was over two months ago. He appeared to have slimmed down and gotten more ripped. Is he working out at the gym or home? More importantly, was there anyone else in his life but you?

"There's only one woman in my life, and that's you." He shook his head and gave me a wide smile when I inquired.

Even though it was ridiculous, I was glad he said it. Given

his age, he should have at least one female companion. A person of his age group. He would be driven by strong desires. Then I had a flashback of Tom. As a teenager, he shared Paul's age. After all, I was much older than him, but at the Dogging site, he was content. As a result, the girlfriend of my son need not be a teenager; she could be a middle-aged or elderly woman.

Seeing him for the first time in a long time seemed like a fresh start. He had the same rugged features as his father, and he was very attractive. I realized that if he wasn't my Son, I'd be the first one in line to have sex with him if he weren't.

We had sex that night. It was a sweet and passionate affair, as usual. Park was fast asleep when we were done, but I was wide awake because I couldn't stop thinking about everything. Paul was at the forefront of my thoughts.

Meeting that young man, the one who looked so much like

my Son, had been a horrible idea. When we had sex, I made things worse by pretending that he was Paul. After that fateful encounter, I realized how much I wanted him!

My feelings for him grew even stronger two days later, perhaps because he was staying with us. My heart races whenever he gets close to me or smiles at me. When I'm in love, I feel like a teenager for the first time. I don't want to be in this state of mind any longer. Before I do something stupid, I need to put an end to this. It was, however, far easier said than accomplished.

By the time the weekend rolled around, it was almost too much. It was time to take action. I was going to lose my mind if I didn't.

I couldn't just ignore it, therefore there were only two options for dealing with it. When it came to my plans, one of them was to entice my son. However, that was a step too far for me at the time. Then if I attempted to meet him, and he rejected me, I would be humiliated. The alternative would have to be considered. In the woods, I planned to screw Tom, the young man who reminded me of my Son. For as long as it took to get rid of my Paul-obsession, I would keep doing it. In the end, things would return to normal, and I might even find this time amusing in hindsight. I'm hoping so because it's been a long time since it's been fun.

So I was on my way to the Dogging site in the woods on Monday night. Park had believed me when I said I was seeing Rita and had agreed to go out with me. But my pal wasn't there, so I was on my own. She'd wanted to come, but she was sick.

A good fuck would be nice but the lucky man who gets to push his cock deep into my small pussy would not be thrilled if I puke on him.

Contrary to popular belief, the majority of Doggers are

respectable human beings. They mingle with like-minded individuals, engage in sexual activity, and then depart. However, you occasionally get a poor fruit. Someone who is disrespectful of others' limits or even violent in their actions. Although it's quite unlikely, you should proceed with caution just in case. In order to avoid doing this alone, I usually go Dogging with a friend of mine. One of us can aid the other if he or she is having a problem. The rate at which they want to have sex was so intense that I took a risk tonight. I broke one of my rules, an important one, but perhaps it won't be a poor decision.

After five minutes of parking, I began to question whether or not I had made the right decision to come here on my own.

While approaching the car, he appeared innocent enough, but when I rolled down the window, his true colors emerged.

He told me what he was going to do to me after holding my hand forcefully and pulling it away from me. Nothing about it appeals to me. In addition to being uncomfortable, it would be excruciatingly painful in that situation. I was frightened, but I didn't want him to know.

Then I added, "Or I could just kill you and consume your liver with some fava beans and a nice Chianti," which I said in a low voice, but one that was full of menace.

Despite the fact that it scared him, he didn't let go of my hand. However, as I looked into his eyes and then smiled, he reciprocated my feelings.

After shaking his head and exclaiming, "You're a crazy motherfucker," he walked away.

However, it was all a facade. However, he didn't realize that I wasn't a particularly aggressive person. Moreover, even if I could have killed him, I wouldn't have done so because I don't enjoy liver.

I took a few long breaths to get myself back to a calm state. If I left, I would've had to return here the following night, which was not an option. Having my son satisfied an unmet need in my life. If that wasn't an option, Tom was the greatest alternative. I just had a feeling he'd be here tonight, and that was all. A great time would be had by all, and then I'd tell him that I wanted more. I was looking for someone to spend time with. I desired the flexibility of being able to visit him whenever the mood struck me. And I wasn't about to accept a no for an answer, either. Rather than turn down his advances or refuse to give him money, I was prepared to do everything he asked of me.

It simply took a few minutes for me to get over that weird individual. I felt like a lady again, one who exuded self-assurance. However, I'll admit that seeing another man walk approach the automobile gave me the willies.

Despite the fact that his head was bowed and he was wearing a sweatshirt, I recognized him as Tom. I swung the door open as soon as he was within striking distance of the vehicle. He got in swiftly. As I turned the light on, I couldn't help but catch my gaze on him.

Neither of us could believe what we were seeing. I got a lot more than I bargained for. To my surprise, Tom, a proxy for my son, had arrived in the woods to meet me!

Just staring into one another's eyes, we couldn't think of anything to say. When faced with a circumstance like this, what do you say?

Then, without warning, he jumped out of the car and ran. I began to weep as I watched him leave. The fact that my son was aware of my dogging activities made me realize that what I'd been doing wasn't glamorous, it was simply sleazy. And to make matters worse, my darling Paul was just as bad as I was. He was a dogger, too.

31

I nearly jumped out of my skin when I heard a tap on the window. If I was confronted by the same man, I was prepared to kill and eat his liver.

However, it turned out to be Paul, so I opened the door for him.

"We might as well talk about it now and get it out of the way," he said.

That was very mature of him, as well as being sensible. When he saw my tears, he was moved. I thanked him with a huge smile as he wiped them with a tissue.

"It's my first time," I respond.

When caught, everyone says that, but I didn't believe him because he was my son. My chance had finally come, but should I tell the truth? It was time for me to be honest with myself.

I've done this before. It's something I've done for years.

His mother's story was a lot to take in, and it took him a while to speak again.

Is there a specific reason for what you do?

That was a straightforward question to ask. I was going to tell him the truth, and I wasn't going to tone it down in any way.

It's a lot of fun. I'm a fan of sex. I enjoy being fucked by a wide variety of cocks.

I knew by the look on his face that I'd gone too far when he looked at me. Nothing could be done about what I'd stated, however. His smile returned.

"Wow, that was a lot to take in."

As for you, "So, how was it for you?"

I'm a nineteen-year-old pussycat who can't stop chasing

pussycats. Anything is fair game for me. "

"Anything?"

He gave a sigh of agreement.

Is it even possible to fuck with your mother?

He was supposed to chuckle since it was a joke. He was not, and it was not for the reasons you might expect. He was taking it very seriously.

My body reacted immediately to his yes. That's when my heart started racing and my pussy began to drool. Even so, I remained in command.

A bad idea, to put it mildly.

"It's true," he said.

Because he said that, I let my guard down and was surprised when he put his hand on my breast and found my nipple. It wasn't until then that I realized I could have avoided it. My nipple had swelled by the time I realized what was happening.

Suddenly, he had his other hand on me as well. Even though it was just a few inches away from my pussy, the sensation was the same as if it were right up there.

I lowered the hood of his jacket when he approached me so that we could kiss. He was a tall, dark, and beautiful man with a strong sense of self. But he wanted me over all the other women. But it wasn't as bad as I had hoped.

My T-shirt was open, and his hand, which had previously been on the outside, was now trying to get into my bra as we kissed. He was having a hard time since I'm a big woman and the bra was too tight.

I could tell he was worried when I stopped kissing him, and I knew exactly why. He was under the impression that we were going to come to an end. That was ridiculous; I couldn't possibly stop now, no matter how hard I tried. The way we were going about things was incorrect. In doing so, we had crossed a line that should never have been crossed. ' That didn't bother me. He'd fuck me to the best climax I've ever had when his cock was deep in my delicious pussy and he was done.

"My top and bra need to come off."

His face was a picture. In its place was an infectious smile. Laughing would have been inappropriate because he wouldn't get the joke.

This was much better, as he was no longer interested in kissing me because of my large breasts. Instead, he opted to lick my nipple with his tongue.

I helped him switch nipples by sliding my breast towards his lips as he lifted his head to do so. Sucking hard and long was his way of saying thank you to me. I screamed out in pain as a result. It sounded more like something made by animals than by people. He wasn't ignoring the other one either. His fingers were devoted to that breast, which was receiving the utmost care.

"Feel free to spread your limbs."

Even though I knew what I was doing was wrong, I went ahead and did it anyway. Rather than touch my knee this time, he placed his hand on my right leg. I was trembling with fear as I wondered what would happen next.

My pussy got even drenched when his hand began to move slowly upwards. His fingers were inches away from the hem of my slacks when I realized what he was doing to me. As I waited for them to cross the threshold, my heart rate quickened and my blood pressure dropped. Then I had to take a deep breath to catch my breath since his hand was moving away from my pussy, not towards it.

"This isn't right," I say.

That was true, but he couldn't afford to second guess himself at this point. Nothing could have prepared me for the heat that was engulfing my genital region. Putting his balls in my pussy was all it took to put out the fires in the inferno that was my life. We had no intention of slowing down!

No problem, I'd like it if you could finger me. "

Unfortunately, that didn't work, either. His hand, which had been wedged between my thighs, was now guiding me to the front door. Something else had to be said before it was too late, something that would compel him to stay.

Then I'll inform your father.

That was pathetic, but it was all I had, and I wouldn't tell him for fear of embarrassing myself in front of him. There was no way that I could do it without him also discovering that I was a dogger. Despite this, the door had been reopened, at least for the time being.

"It's ridiculous. I know you wouldn't do that," I said.

It's true, but could you please stay? "

After that, I pounded him with my heavy artillery. If that wasn't enough, I burst into tears to make him notice my wide-open eyes. He hugged me, which was exactly how I expected him to behave.

I muttered in his ear as he held me, my teeth squished against his chest.

"The only thing your mother wants you to do is to touch her dripping moist pussy." The question is whether or not you'll be a nice lad and follow through. "

Even though I was nervous about him not saying "Yes Mummy," my joy was extinguished by the fact that he eventually said so.

His hand didn't stop when it reached the hem of my pants as it moved between my legs this time. His fingers were now pressing against them as he searched for the softest spot in my crotch. My clit is the crowning glory. When he finally found it, he was able to tell because I was moaning so loudly. As soon as he started rubbing it, the noise got even worse. This was fine, but it would have been even better if he had pointed a finger at me instead.

"I need some fingers deep in my pussy, so take down my pants."

He started yanking my bottom down as soon as I lifted it. He had them all the way down to my ankles and then removed them.

That's what happened to me this time. I'd requested "some" fingers in my pussy, and he'd graciously given me three instead of the two I'd requested. Because he didn't tell me, I'm not going to complain about it. Paul had found it amusing that when I gasped in return, my reaction had been to laugh.

His other hand now had two fingers on my crotch. When the fingers in my pussy began to move, it was even more lovely.

It made me happy to see how well he could manipulate a woman's body just by moving his fingers. And I did not doubt that he'd be great at fucking as well, but that would have to wait until after he'd successfully seduced me.

While having a good time with a pussy, most young men tend to get a little overexcited and start acting like jerks. There is too much movement of their fingers and too much rubbing of that delicate little stone. That's not true for my son. Compared to Park, he was a natural at this, and I was impressed. All of his actions toward me were excellent. He was gradually escalating the tension. I was having a good time on the road, but the greatest part was yet to come.

That wasn't too far off, either! My breathing was labored, and my pussy was alerting me that I was about to arrive. That's exactly what happened seconds later, and with a ferocity, I didn't expect. It was exhausting to the point where I almost passed out at its height.

Most of the time, I need to cum twice, and on rare occasions, three times, before I'm satisfied. However, in order for me to fully recuperate, I require some time in between. However, not tonight. Immediately after the first one was finished, I was anxious for more.

"Let go of your cock now, it was amazing." It's time to fuck me. "

It was all over his face. When he heard the news, he looked like a kid in a toy store who had just learned he could get whatever he wanted!

His fingers and thumbs were all that was left of him as he tried to remove his jeans. He did it as if it were the first time. I tried not to laugh, but it was difficult. They took off at some point. He didn't have to worry about his pants.

Looking at what I was getting, I could tell by my smile that I was content. My best guess is that it was roughly an inch longer than his father's. That said, it was nonetheless amazing in a different way. It was more substantial than a typical cock.

"Would you like to share your thoughts?"

With his confident tone, he was expecting my approval. And I was pleased to oblige, as it was a lovely cock.

"That's a good one," I first said. "I like it a lot," after a second glance.

My pussy was begging to be fucked, but it would have to wait, for I now needed his cock in my scrotum. In lieu of asking him whether it was his preference, I simply descended my shoulders and looked away. He couldn't possibly say no to his mother's offer to suck his swollen member.

His cock's head was covered in my full lips. I was taking my time to savor every bite. It was unnecessary to hurry.

"This is fantastic," said the audience.

It was only the beginning; things were going to get much better from here. My attention was drawn to him by a glint in the corner of my eye. He had his chin pressed against the glass of the window as if he were mocking me. Because he was opening the window, Paul had noticed him too. The man retreated when it began to fall. Tom was the culprit.

There's room for one more person.

I shook my head as I continued to serve Paul's chicken. Since my son was with me, I no longer needed him at the dogging site.

"Sorry, the lady has said no."

He wasn't expecting such a response. His smile had faded and he appeared to be enraged now.

"She's nothing but a slut." She wants to have sex with her child. "

It's time for him to leave now that he's finished speaking. He didn't move, though.

"Your options are as follows: leaving is an option, or I'll get out of the car and sever your head off." Stop pressuring me to do it. "

He'd said it matter-of-factly and casually. Tom, if you're

reading this, I recommend that you fuck off while you're still conscious. It was as if he had his tail between his legs, and so he did.

In my mouth, there was an enormously fat chicken that I couldn't laugh at.

I was able to push him over the edge in no time. I was an experienced performer who had put in a lot of time and effort. I was a master of the cock sucker. And once I had him there, I was determined to keep him there for as long as possible. After a few seconds of bouncing my head, I saw that it was completely motionless. He could get there with the tiniest nudge.

"Put an end to this for me."

As much as he wanted to come, he'd be waiting a little longer now.

"I beg of you, please."

It would be cruel to keep him from reaching his zenith for much longer. He came as I bobbed my head and tried to take in as much of his charm as I could. As he spits it into my mouth, I gulped it down, and when he finished, I licked the cock clean off of it. The flavor of cumin is one of my favorites!

It was the nicest blowjob I've ever received.

Did I make a mistake by saying that? It's going to be a long time before he can get hard again, which is a bummer. I couldn't help but smile. There was a pussy waiting for his cock when he was nineteen. Getting him ready for sex wasn't a big deal.

Seeing that I was correct was a pleasant surprise. It had already been raised to its full height when I arrived.

"What are your plans?"

A true gentleman would allow the lady to make her own

decision. Because of the heat, there is no lady in me tonight; instead, I am a scorched bitch.

As soon as I stated, "I want you to fuck me from behind," he was stunned.

"Are you f*cking serious?"

I nodded and shook my head in agreement.

To do so has always been a goal of mine, and tonight I'm ready to make it happen.

"We could always try again."

"No, you can't do that. Do as your mother tells you to. "

Then he said: "OK, but don't hold me responsible if it all goes terribly wrong."

We had exited the vehicle and were now on the sidewalk. Fucking me on the grass was all I wanted from him. This is my first time doing something like this. In the past, I'd gone dogging a lot, but I'd always stayed in the vehicle.

There's no reason why we couldn't do it here.

He was directing his attention to the back of the automobile.

"It's not possible to see us from here."

That's why I decided to go with this one. We're all going to be able to see each other, aren't we? "

"That's," he said, pausing for a few moments to mull on the appropriate adjective to characterize it.

"Outrageous."

I couldn't help but chuckle. I said, "I'm done," and when I was done, "Your father and I are going to have sex with you." That's just plain ridiculous. Everything else pales in comparison to that. "

So when I pointed to the location where I wanted to do it,

he didn't say anything, and so I interpreted it as a yes when he wasn't saying anything.

It was right in front of the car. I removed my skirt before crawling down on all fours.

"Remove your shirt and socks."

As a result, both of us were now completely naked.

"We've caught the attention of a few folks." If you don't want them to participate, please let me know as soon as possible. "

Even for me, that was a bit much, but I was tempted to taunt him by saying that I was game. To avoid freaking him out, I could tell him that I wanted as many of them to participate as possible, but it would be too much. By telling him the truth, I was able to put him at ease.

It's just the two of us now. Watch, but don't touch them, I

tell them.

He appeared to be relieved as he walked away. Some of the onlookers approached us as he walked behind me. One of them had already had his crotch yanked.

I stepped in because Paul was supposed to be the one to explain the rules, but he was silent.

Let me show you how we do it. Then again, that's all there is. There will be no physical contact. "

When you say, "I want to fuck you, too," it's unfair.

One of the men rescued me before I could finish my sentence.

"That will not happen." When a lady says "no, she means no."

I could see why that silenced him. He said it softly because he didn't need to shout when you're that big. He towered over the rest of the group. He was more than capable of dealing with anyone who got out of line.

Paul's brake wasn't as hard as it should have been when he drove into me. That made sense to me. He was apprehensive because we were in front of an audience.

"Imagine that I'm your mother and close your eyes."

Some of the onlookers chuckled, but would they have laughed if they knew I was his mother?

A few strokes later, it was back to its former glory, and the added thickness of his cock was stretching my pussy.

A bitch, that one.

I interpreted it as a kind word.

In my opinion, she's the real deal.

That's a point I can't dispute. It's safe to say I was a whore when I was fucked by my son in front of strangers at a dogging site.

He should have her as his mother because she's old enough.

I mumbled to myself, "I wish my girlfriend were like her."

When one of the men said, "Amen to that," everyone laughed.

Most of the men surrounding us were now stroking their cocks while they watched and talked.

Make my life a misery. Make your mother cum for you. "

Do your best since the narcissist expects you to work hard.

This was exactly what I'd hoped for in a sexual experience. A group of people was watching as my son's cock did beautiful things to my pussy. I put on the best performance of my life as the center of attention.

My presence here today would not have been possible if my partner had been moaning like that in bed with me.

That was echoed by a few of the men.

"Fuck, I'll be right there."

I'm relieved that it wasn't my son saying that. A couple more strokes would have made the difference.

"Put an end to this for me."

When you're done with her, you can pour your hot coffee into her cup and finish her off.

Paul was now putting in his all-out effort to see that through. He was fucking me so hard that he nearly pushed me over. I was lifting my bottom as high as I could with both of his hands on my hips. No cock, not even his father's, had ever fucked me harder or gone deeper into me than this.

My small pussy cum, thanks to my son's cock. I yelled as soon as I got there.

What happened after that is a bit of a mystery. When I dropped to the ground, I saw the stars, but other than that, I had no recollection of what had happened. As soon as I opened my eyes again, the men were still standing in front of me. They began clapping as Paul pulled me to my feet. As soon as I got to my feet, I gave my audience a great dramatic bow, which made them all laugh out loud. After that, they began to scatter. One of them said something to the effect of, "Goodbye."

"Will we see you then?"

While we were outside, we changed our clothes. There should be some remorse or maybe guilt now that we'd done it and I'd had my fill of you. However, nothing like that happened. My life felt complete, both as an individual and as a woman. "I was one with the universe" would have been my answer if I had been a sixties hippie. That, though, was absurd; all I was thinking about was how amazing I felt.

Despite this, Paul remained meek. He could feel remorseful.

"Is there anything you'd like to add?"

He paused for a moment before responding to my question, and then responded, "It wasn't bad at all." The problem is that there's so much to learn. *My mother and I have had sex*. If that wasn't horrible enough, it was done in front of a crowd of people at a dog-grooming establishment.

What's the matter? Do we do it again? " I inquired.

Of course, I do, but why don't we meet at my place or yours next time? It'll be a lot safer and more comfortable to perform it in that location.

I shake my head and then say, "I don't know." "No, I'm your mother, and you should treat me with respect while we're not at the dogging site." You may treat me like a whore here because I'm a bitch. "

Before he left, he gave me a sweet kiss on the lips and hugged me. That re-ignited my pulse.

When I got home, I was surprised to see Park still awake, and he appeared to be crying. What had transpired worried me.

A huge mistake has been made on my part. Honestly, I don't know why I did it. "

In his natural state, he was a very calm person; nothing could get him to this level of anxiety. Was he responsible for the death of someone?

I'd like to know what you've accomplished.

"To park, I went. I've been doing a lot of dogging. "

His face contorted into a stoic expression. When I saw this, I couldn't help but laugh. Suddenly, he appeared perplexed.

"I'm going to tell you where and what I have been doing." was my parting statement after finishing.

Afterward, I told him everything but used Tom instead of Paul as the narrator. Until I finished, he didn't utter a word.

"Wow, I think we should go together next time around." However, Paul should not be aware of this. "

I gave a nod of approval. Dogging was no longer my dirty little secret; I now had a new one to keep hidden from everyone.

My son has become my most heinous secret!

Acknowledgements

The Glory of this book success goes to God Almighty and my beautiful Family, Fans, Readers & well-wishers, Customers, and Friends for their endless support and encouragement.

About The Author

I've been writing romance novels for almost eight years. As an erotica fanatic and author, I create erotica that is dark and romantic. I love the force of darkness and the sexiness that comes with it, so I write dark and sexy romance. I've always enjoyed romance novels, and now I'm writing them as well. Nothing excites me more than the prospect of you reading and appreciating my fiction as much as I like stretching the boundaries of sexual pleasure in my work.